SQUISH
BOOM
tap
Squeak
tap
BA-BOOM
SQUISH
click
Thump
tap

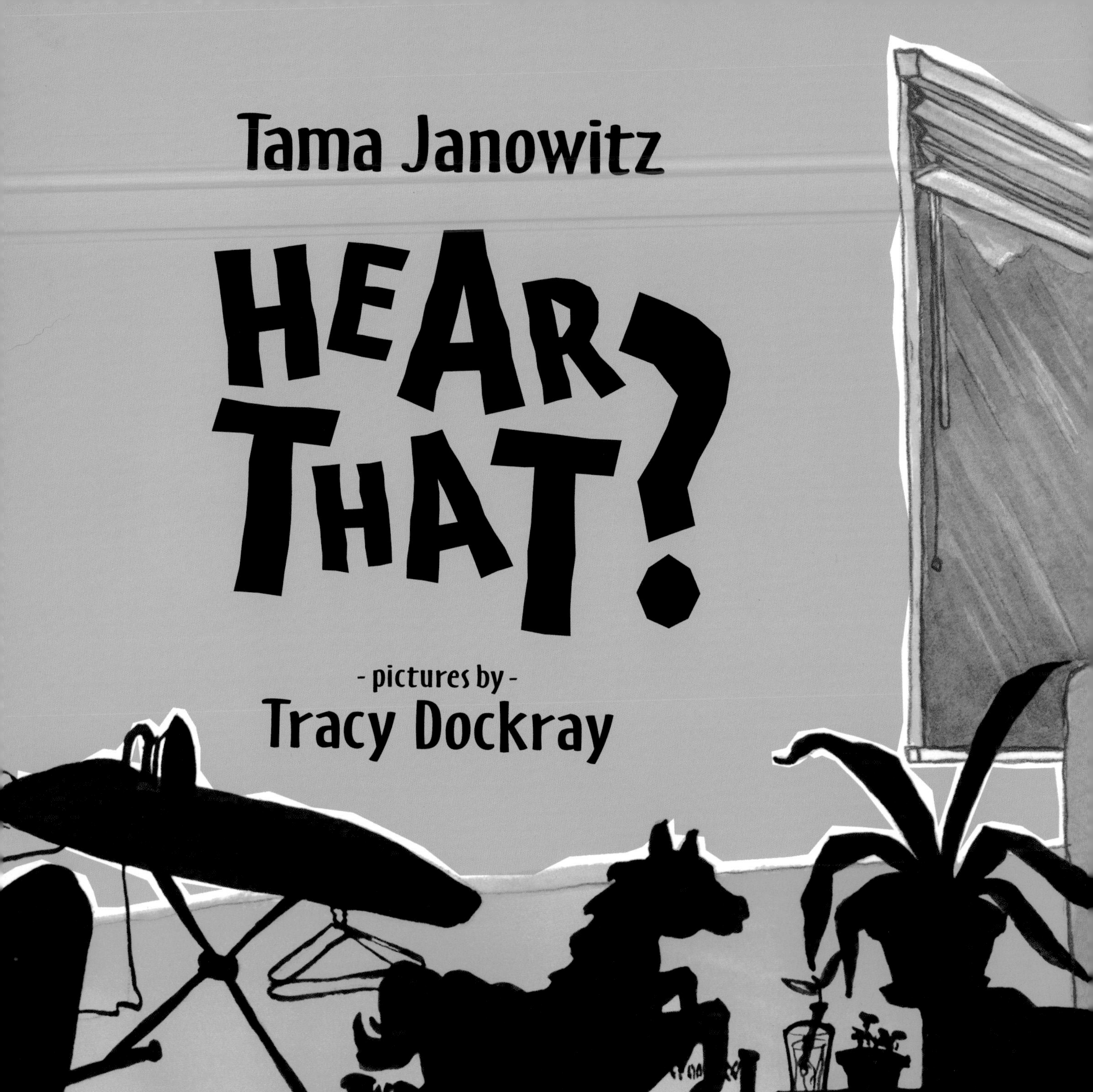

Tama Janowitz

HEAR THAT?

- pictures by -

Tracy Dockray

SeaStar Books
New York

Mom and I were alone at home.

"Ssshhh," I said. "Hear THAT?"

"Yes," said Mom. "Maybe it's Daddy."

BUZZ
BUZZZ
BUZZZ

"No," I said.
"Daddy doesn't go
BUZZ, BUZZ, BUZZ.
Maybe a fruit fly."

"No," said Mom. "Hear THAT?

A fly doesn't go
SQUEAK, SQUEAK, SQUEAK."

"Maybe a mouse," I said.
"A mouse munching
on cracker crumbs
under my covers."

"No," said Mom. "Hear THAT?

SQUISH
SQUISH
SQUIS

Mice don't go
SQUISH, SQUISH, SQUISH."

"Maybe the butler," I said.
"Stepping on that old banana."

"No," said Mom. "Hear THAT?

click
click
click

We don't have a butler
that goes CLICK, CLICK, CLICK."

"Maybe sugar ants," I said. "A million sugar ants
swarming around the strawberry jelly."

"No," said Mom. "Hear THAT?

tap tap tap
tap tap tap
tap tap tap tap
tap tap tap tap ta
tap tap
tap tap tap tap

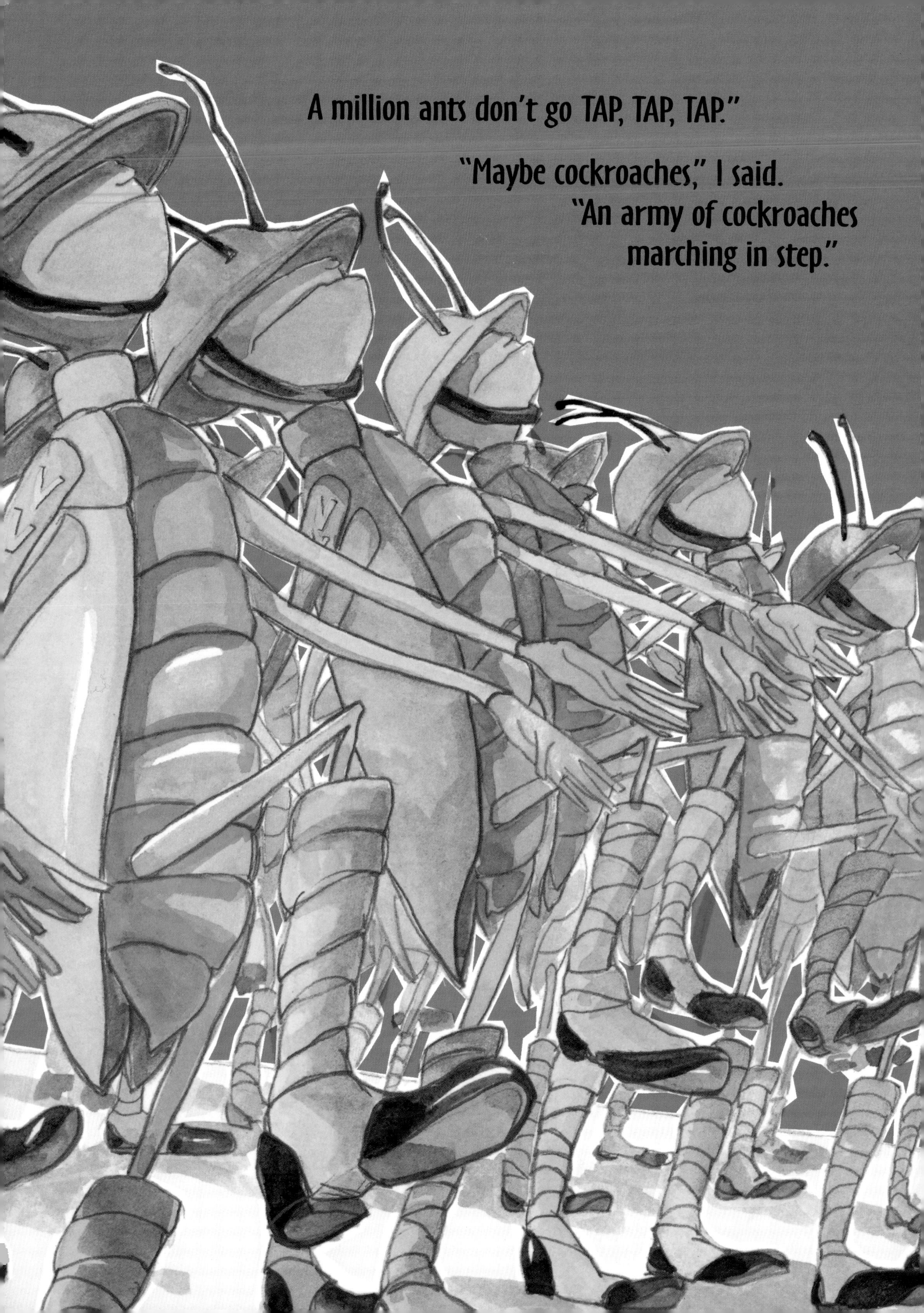

A million ants don't go TAP, TAP, TAP."

"Maybe cockroaches," I said.
"An army of cockroaches
marching in step."

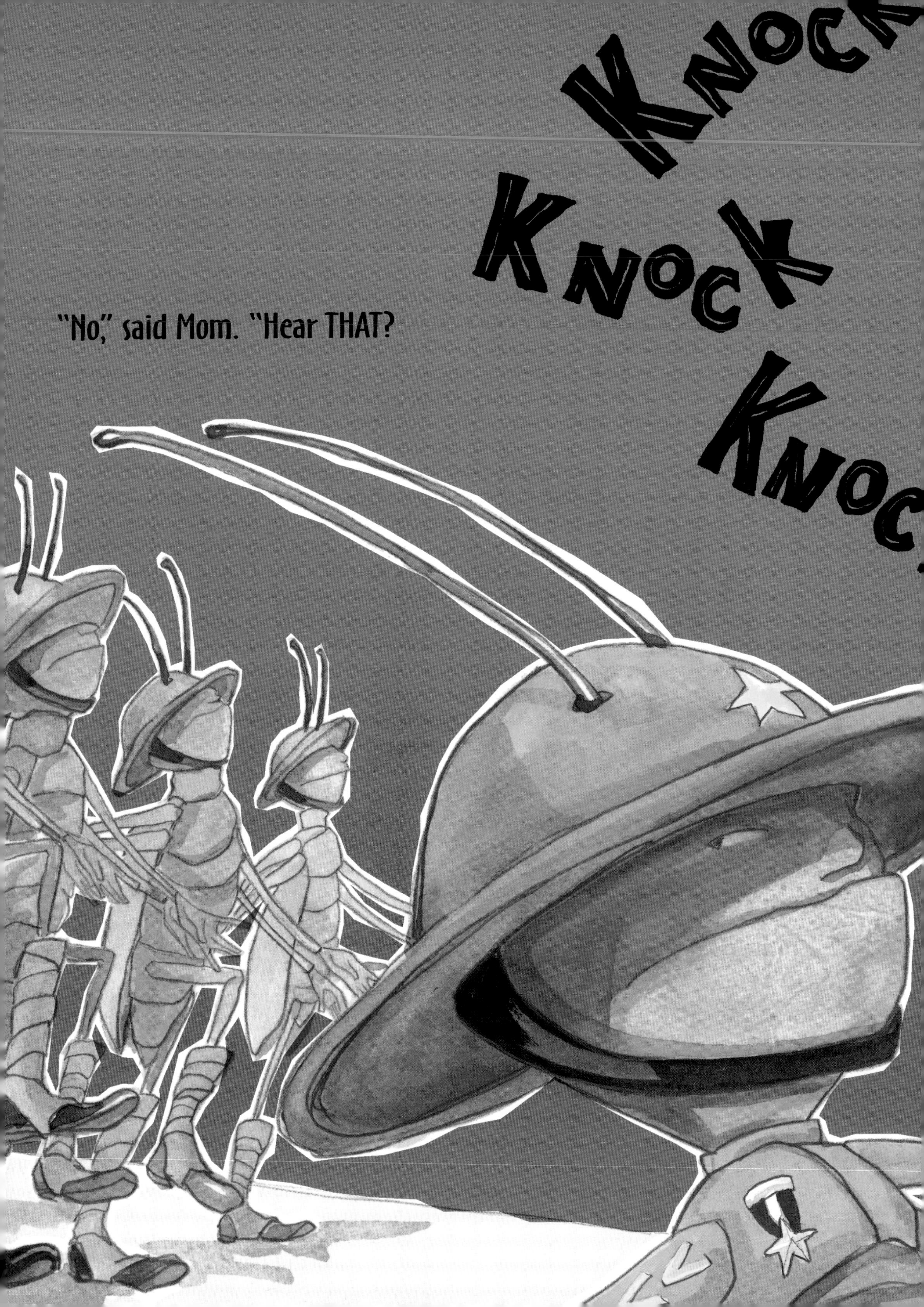
KNOCK
KNOCK
"No," said Mom. "Hear THAT?
KNOC

An army of cockroaches
can't go
KNOCK,
KNOCK,
KNOCK."

"Maybe it's that
old banana," I said.
"Banging on my closet,
where I left his peel."

"No, silly," said Mom.
"Hear THAT?

Thump
Thump
Thump
Thump

Bananas don't go THUMP, THUMP, THUMP!"

"Maybe it's our wombat," I said. "Going through the smelly garbage in the kitchen."

"Perhaps," said Mom. "Or even our kangaroos!"

"I know," I said.
"It's the walrus I put in the refrigerator.

Or even that
horrible,
hairy
ginip-ginop!

Trying to
escape . . .

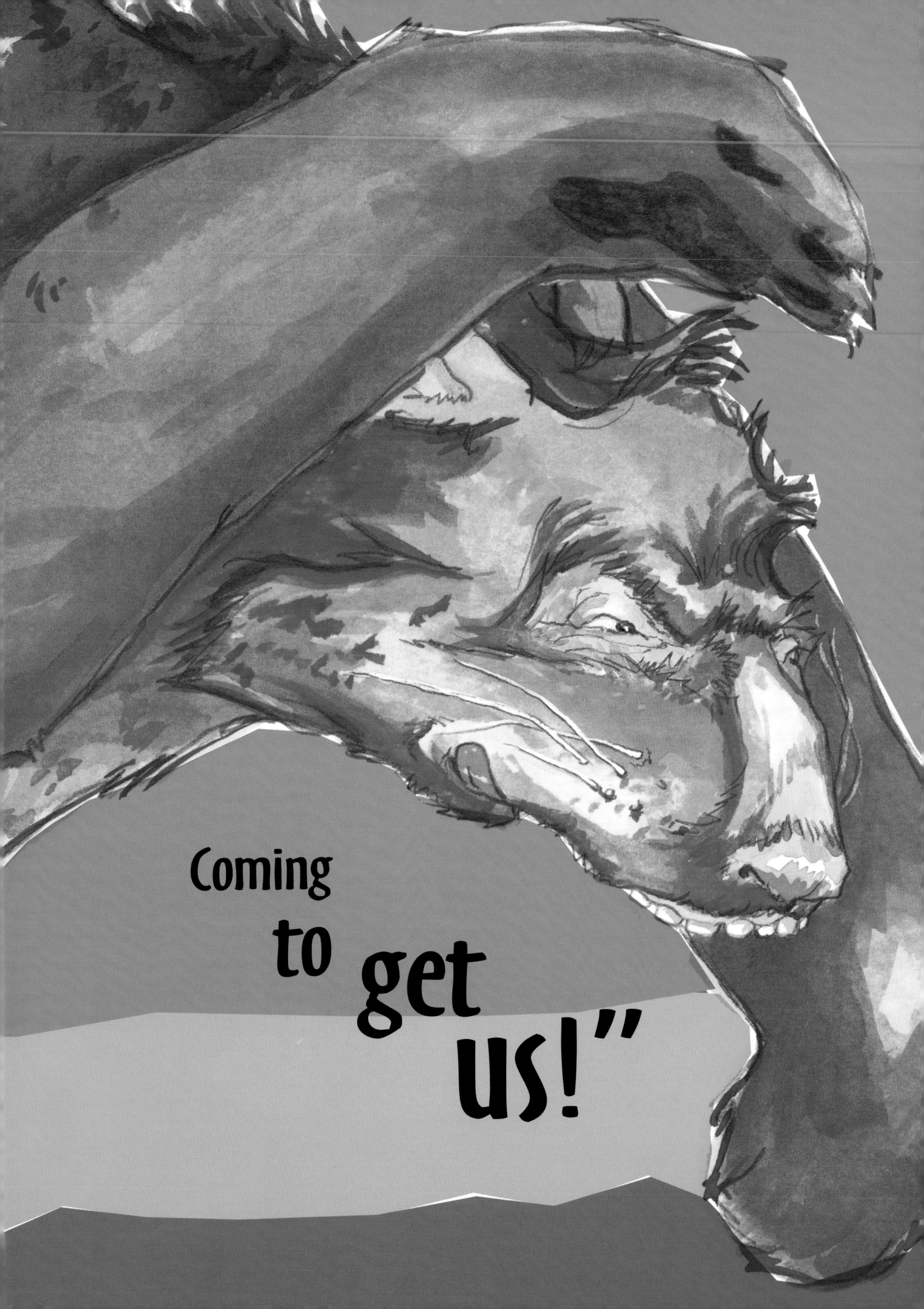
Coming
to get
us!”

BOOM
BA-

"No," said Mom.
"Everyone knows ginip-ginops don't go
BOOM,
BA-BOOM,
BA-BOOM!"

"Maybe we should go look," I said.
"I'll protect you."

"No ginip-ginops in here," said Mom.
"Or wombats,
walruses,
bananas,
or butlers."

"It looks like they were," I said.
"They must be hiding."

"Yes," said Mom. "Hear THAT?"

"What else," I said,
"could go

Squeak
Squish Squish
Thump Knock
Knock
Buzz Buzz Thump
Buzz Thump
tap
tap
tap

EXCEPT—

"DADDY!"

"I knew it was you, Daddy," I said,
"but Mom was a little scared.

She thought you were
a fruit fly,
and a mouse,
and a butler,
and a million sugar ants,
and an army of cockroaches,
and a banana,
and a wombat,
and a walrus,
and even
a hairy
ginip-ginop!"

"Ssshhh," said Daddy.

"Hear THAT?"

Design by David Andrew DiRienz

SeaStar Books
A division of North-South Books Inc.

First published in the United States by SeaStar Books,
a division of North-South Books Inc., New York.
Published simultaneously in Canada, Australia,
and New Zealand by North-South Books,
an imprint of Nord-Süd Verlag AG, Gossau Zürich, Switzerland.

Library of Congress Cataloging-in-Publication Data is available.

The art for this book was prepared using watercolors, Adobe Illustrator, and Adobe Photoshop.
The text for this book is set in Bitstream Oz Handicraft.

ISBN 1-58717-074-4 (trade binding)
1 3 5 7 9 TB 10 8 6 4 2

ISBN 1-58717-075-2 (library binding)
1 3 5 7 9 TB 10 8 6 4 2

Printed by Proost NV in Belgium

For more information about our books,
and the authors and artists who create them,
visit our web site: www.northsouth.com

For Willow Hunt — T.J.

To Andrea, who creates
order from chaos — T.D.

Knock

Thump

click

tap

SQUISH

Squeak

BUZZZZ